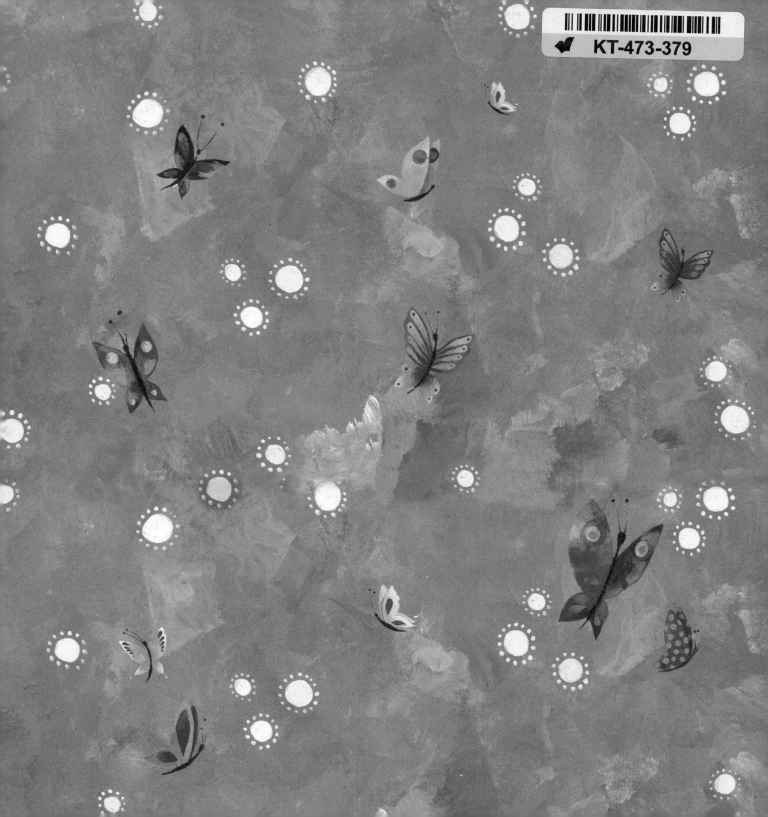

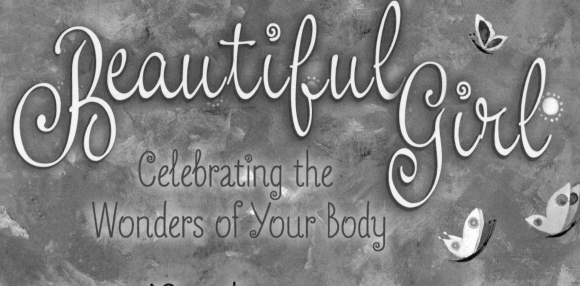

Beautiful Girl

Celebrating the Wonders of Your Body

Christiane Northrup, M.D., with Kristina Tracy

illustrated by
Aurélie Blanz

HAY HOUSE, INC.
Carlsbad, California • New York City
London • Sydney • New Delhi

Published in the United States by: Hay House, Inc.: www.hayhouse.com • *Published in Australia by:* Hay House Australia Pty. Ltd.: www.hayhouse.com.au • *Published in the United Kingdom by:* Hay House UK, Ltd.: www.hayhouse.co.uk • *Published in India by:* Hay House Publishers India: www.hayhouse.co.in

Cover and interior design and editorial assistance: Jenny Richards • *Illustrations:* © Aurélie Blanz

Library of Congress Control Number: 2011920902

ISBN: 978-1-4019-3403-3
Digital ISBN: 978-1-4019-3404-0

15   14   13   12   11   10   9   8   7   6
1st edition, January 2013

Printed in the United States of America

SUSTAINABLE FORESTRY INITIATIVE
Certified Chain of Custody
Promoting Sustainable Forestry
www.sfiprogram.org
SFI-01268

SFI label applies to the text stock

Dear Parents,

I have spent my career helping women get healthy and stay healthy through proper diet, exercise, medicine, and a positive attitude about their bodies. Out of all of these things, I have come to realize that the most important part of a woman's health is her attitude about her body. With *Beautiful Girl*, your little girl can start loving her body right here and now! Having a deep and unshakable belief that her body is beautiful and contains powerful creative magic is a little girl's birthright. Knowing this will set the stage for her physical and mental health throughout her life.

Most adult women have received some negative messages about their bodies, which can show up later in life as health problems or unhealthy behavior. This needn't be the case. When little girls grow up knowing that their bodies are perfect and miraculous, they are far more likely to grow into happy and healthy adult women. That is why Kristina Tracy and I wrote *Beautiful Girl*. It is our sincere hope that this book will be a starting point in a much longer conversation between you and your daughter, and that its message will help her internalize a positive body image that will lead to a lifetime of vibrant health and happiness.

Christiane Northrup, M.D.

Hello, beautiful girl.
Do you know how lucky you are?
Why? Because you were born a girl!
And as a girl, you have been given special gifts
that will bloom as you do.

These special gifts are just for girls!
Boys have their own.
Right now you are probably too young
to understand all the amazing
things your body can do,
but as you grow up, you
will begin to notice them.

Think of your body like
a magical garden—always growing
and changing, full of color and life.

And just as a garden has much to explore
and discover, your body is filled with
wonderful secrets that you
will learn in time.

Everything in nature is
perfect just the way it is.

Each little seed sprouts up differently
in its own time and its own way.
You are the same—
perfect just the way you are!

A garden is filled with delicate plants
and tiny creatures.
As you walk among them,
you are careful with them.
You should be just as careful with your own body.
Treat it gently and make sure others treat it gently, too.
Don't let anyone touch you
in a way that does not feel right.
This is your precious body—
trust your feelings!

There is a lot that comes along with being a girl, and sometimes your body will surprise you. Don't worry or be embarrassed about the changes you see and feel—every girl on Earth will experience similar things. And remember, you can always talk to an older girl or woman that you trust if you have questions.

Imagine yourself lying on a
soft blanket of grass in the warm sun.
Doesn't it feel good on your skin?

Your body is made to enjoy all sorts of
good feelings, and as you get older
they will get stronger. This is just
nature's way of telling you that
you are growing up.

Over time things about you will start to change.
These changes will happen slowly and will give you
a glimpse of the woman you will become.

Tadpoles become frogs
        and caterpillars turn into butterflies,
        and you will become
                who you are meant to be.

You have a special strength inside of you.
It is there to help with all of the important things
you will need to do in your life.
Know that you are like a magnificent tree—
your roots hold strong in any weather, and your
branches and leaves are a shelter
for those you love.

Someday you may decide to become a mother yourself.
And because you were born a beautiful girl,
        you already have a little nest inside of you.
This nest waits and grows and prepares
        for the time when you are ready to create a new life.
It is a miracle, just like you are a miracle!

Every girl on Earth
    is special and unique.
Yes, you are one of a kind,
    but at the same time you are a
part of something bigger—
all the women and girls; mothers,
daughters, and sisters
    who bring their magical gifts
    to the world.

The End

This book is dedicated to all the beautiful girls in the world, both young and old. Take care of your precious body and it will take care of you.

— Christiane Northrup